BRIDGE A PULL OF EMOTIONS

NAVIGATING EMOTIONAL WATERS

MUDIT SRIVASTAVA

BLUEROSE PUBLISHERS
India | U.K.

Copyright © Mudit Srivastava 2024

All rights reserved by author. No part of this publication may be reproduced, stored in a retrieval system or transmitted in any form or by any means, electronic, mechanical, photocopying, recording or otherwise, without the prior permission of the author. Although every precaution has been taken to verify the accuracy of the information contained herein, the publisher assumes no responsibility for any errors or omissions. No liability is assumed for damages that may result from the use of information contained within.

BlueRose Publishers takes no responsibility for any damages, losses, or liabilities that may arise from the use or misuse of the information, products, or services provided in this publication.

For permissions requests or inquiries regarding this publication, please contact:

BLUEROSE PUBLISHERS
www.BlueRoseONE.com
info@bluerosepublishers.com
+91 8882 898 898
+4407342408967

ISBN: 978-93-5989-749-3

Cover design: Rishav Rai
Typesetting: Rohit

First Edition: January 2024

Acknowledgement

To my dearest family and friends,

Your unwavering support has been the backbone of "Bridge: A Pull of Emotions." Thank you for tolerating my countless hours lost in words and worlds. Your encouragement fueled my creativity.

A special thanks to my editor and the publishing team for shaping my thoughts into a coherent narrative. To the readers, your curiosity and willingness to explore the emotions within "Bridge" mean the world.

This book is dedicated to the magic of storytelling and the connections it forges. Your presence in this journey is my greatest reward.

With heartfelt gratitude, Mudit Srivastava

Contents

The Setup 1

The Meeting 4

Apology 7

First Move 11

The Acceptance 16

The Beginning 21

The Letter 25

The Destiny 28

The Last Ride 32

The *Setup*

Vidhi couldn't contain her curiosity any longer. With a mischievous glint in her eyes, she prodded me to spill the beans on my love story.

"Come on Grandpa, you are blushing like a girl. We are 21st-century children; please tell us your love story. I promise, no one will tease you after your love story," Vidhi insisted, nudging me playfully.

With a smile playing on my lips, I decided to unravel the tale. "Okay, you always wanted to know whom you resemble and why your daddy is so arrogant. See," I said, taking out a secret photo from my wallet, "she is the reason."

Vivan chimed in, dismissing the notion of arrogance. "Mom! What a joke, Dad. She was so cute and humble. How can you call her arrogant?"

Smirking, Vidhi remarked, "Grandmom. She was very beautiful, and I looked very similar to her."

Lost in a world of memories, I nodded. "She was out of this world."

Curious, Vidhi questioned, "Arrogance of what, Grandpa?"

I shared, "She was the daughter of our school's principal, and according to her, no one could stand in front of her. According to her, she was the best."

Vidhi, puzzled, asked, "How can anyone be so rude and arrogant? You are so simple and innocent; on the other hand, she was rude and arrogant? So much difference in behavior—still together, how?"

I explained with a twinkle in my eye, "Opposites attract, dear. She loved showing off, and I believed in simplicity. I love working silently, and my simplicity became the reason for our first meeting."

Excitedly, Vidhi inquired, "So you approached and proposed to her first?"

I chuckled, "Wow… absolutely wrong. Our first meeting was not romantic at all. We met at the school's parking for a fight."

Vidhi burst into laughter. "You and fight! What a joke."

Undeterred, I replied, "What happened, have I told any joke?"

Still giggling, Vidhi managed to say, "You and fighting, that too with a girl, is not less than any joke. I can't believe that you fought with a girl."

I grinned, "Our first meeting is not romantic, but this fight set the base of our love story."

Intrigued, Vidhi leaned forward. "Amazing and interesting. Why and where did you have a fight with the girl in the photo?"

The Meeting

25th November 2000, Delhi Public School (D.P.S)

The atmosphere at D.P.S was charged with tension, the impending pre-board exams casting a shadow over the school grounds. As a dedicated student, I was navigating through the stress when an unexpected encounter disrupted the routine. Shristi, known for her bold demeanor and last-minute approach to academics, became the focal point of an unforeseen confrontation with me.

It was a typical Friday, and the clock was ticking towards 8 AM when the morning tranquility shattered with Shristi's sharp shout. She had taken issue with my Luna being parked in her designated spot, setting the stage for a confrontation that would leave a lasting impact. Despite being caught off guard, I quickly apologized and hurried to my class, hoping to leave the brewing conflict behind.

After School

The echoes of the morning clash lingered as Shristi took an unusual approach to resolve the situation. In a surprising move, she handed me a sum of money, attempting to assert dominance and demand noninterference. Vidhi, my granddaughter, couldn't comprehend Shristi's audacity and questioned my connection to such an apparently arrogant character.

Maintaining composure, I explained the situation to Vidhi, emphasizing the importance of respect. Little did she know that I had responded to Shristi's challenge in a way that would polarize the entire school. A bold proposition was on the table — a challenge to outshine Shristi in the upcoming exams, with the promise of a public apology from her and my departure from the school if I fell short.

The school atmosphere became charged with anticipation as students and even teachers aligned themselves either with me or with the prospect of witnessing Shristi's defeat. Despite my friend

Lucky questioning the sanity of the challenge, my resolve remained unwavering as I faced the impending exams with confidence.

(After the Last Paper)

As the exams concluded, Lucky approached me with a surprising revelation. Unaware of my academic performance, I learned that I had emerged victorious, securing the top position in both sections. A sense of achievement enveloped me as I inquired about the promised surprise.

Lucky, with an air of suspense, revealed the source of the surprise — a gift from Shristi along with a letter expressing remorse for her past behavior. The revelation did little to appease my irritation, but Lucky, ever the mediator, urged me to consider giving Shristi another chance.

Vidhi, curious about my decision, awaited the answer that would shape the next chapter of this unexpected saga.

Apology

I found myself at a crossroads, torn between the logical decisions of my mind and the yearnings of my heart. My perceptive granddaughter, Vidhi, wasted no time in probing the outcome of this internal struggle.

"So, who won, your heart or your brain?" she asked.

Typically guided by reason, I surprised even myself with my response. "Normally, I listen to my brain, but this time, I don't know why I decided to listen to my heart and give her another chance."

Reveling in my uncharacteristic choice, Vidhi expressed her pride. "Wow, Dadaji, I am so proud to be your granddaughter. Do you still have that letter, or do you remember anything written in it?"

I chuckled, a nostalgic gleam in my eyes. "That's great, thank you. I kept all her handwritten letters, and they're still in good condition. Want to see them?"

Bubbling with excitement, Vidhi couldn't resist the opportunity. "Of course, yes! Where have you kept these letters? I am excited to see what was written in the letter that melted your heart. Oh, Dadaji... You are blushing like a girl, so cute."

Dismissing the notion of blushing at my age, I shared a playful moment with Vidhi. "Look at me, Vidhi. I am 88. How can I blush?"

Undeterred, Vidhi appealed to the timeless nature of emotions. "Please don't pass such a platitude; age is just a number. I can understand your condition and your feelings. Just tell me where you stored all her secret letters."

Casually enjoying a chewing gum, I revealed the location of my treasure trove. "Open the locker in my cupboard and take out my silver Sandook. In this silver chest, I kept all her letters and gifts, and you can also see the gift that she gifted me with an apology letter after she came second in school."

Vidhi's excitement reached new heights. "My excitement is now at the next level. Dadaji, can you please read the letter for me again? By the way, what's the code?"

Introducing an element of mystery, I challenged Vidhi to unravel the contents of the cherished box. "You have to open it by cracking the clue, and your clue is LOVE. Open the box and give me the letter in 15 minutes."

Oozing confidence, Vidhi made a bold promise. "15 minutes is more than sufficient for me. I will be in front of you in only five (5) minutes."

Amused by Vidhi's enthusiasm, I couldn't help but draw a familiar comparison. "I like your confidence but remember, there is a very minute difference line between confidence and overconfidence. You are no different from your grandmom as she was always full of confidence."

Determined to prove herself, Vidhi swiftly cracked the code and unveiled the treasure in just over four minutes. "Take it, Dadaji. I have opened your magical Sandook in just 4 minutes and 10 seconds. Now, as a reward, read her apology letter and let me guess why you decided to meet her and give her another chance."

Reminiscing about the past, I began the journey of unraveling memories. "After I came back home from school, the first thing I did was I took out the gift and read the letter. After opening the gift, I couldn't control my laughter."

Intrigued, Vidhi questioned the source of my amusement. "Is there something chucklesome?"

With a twinkle in my eye, I revealed the hidden humor within the gift. "Yes, read what is written in the stick (gift)."

Reading aloud, Vidhi uncovered a simple yet profound message. "'I am stupid and I deserve this.' Oh... so sweet."

Observing Vidhi's emotional response, I teased her gently. "Hey... what happened? Why are these big tear droplets in such cute eyes?"

Touched by the sincerity of the gift, Vidhi had a newfound understanding. "No need to read the letter. Now I understand why you met her and gave her a second chance. I was so wrong about her, but now, seeing this gift, I too give her another chance, as no one is perfect."

Proud of Vidhi's empathy and wisdom, I offered my heartfelt blessings. "I am so proud of you that you, at such a small age, understand anyone's feelings. God bless you, my child."

Curious about the details, Vidhi sought more insights. "Dadaji, where and when did she request you to meet?"

First Move

On the 25th of December, 2000, I hailed an auto, instructing the driver to head towards Dada-Dadi Park. The city buzzed with Christmas cheer as I embarked on a journey that held the promise of a fresh start. The auto driver, a newcomer from Rajasthan, navigated the unfamiliar terrain.

"Auto… bhaiya, Dada-Dadi Park," I instructed.

"Sit, Rs 80 (including parking charges). It will take 40 minutes to reach, and usually, no passenger comes back here," the auto driver informed.

"Okay… proceed. By the way, bhaiya, do you know why this park is called Dada-Dadi Park?" I inquired.

"Sorry sir, I am new here. I came here to work from Rajasthan," the auto driver replied.

"Oh, okay."

Twenty minutes later, the auto pulled up to its destination.

"Sir... reached your destination," the auto driver announced.

"Thank you, bhaiya. Do you have a QR code?" I asked.

"Yes, but it doesn't accept payments less than Rs 100," he informed.

"Okay. Can you drop me back? I'll pay you."

The auto driver smiled, expressing no qualms with his eyes.

"Murmuring to myself, I thought, 'Wow, it's such a beautiful park. Amazing place to meet and make a fresh start.'"

As I immersed myself in the serene ambiance, a familiar voice interrupted my thoughts.

"Hello, Mr. Jeh, turn around, please," said Shristi.

"What a drastic change, Miss Shristi! I hope you don't mind me calling you Miss Shristi," I remarked.

"No issues. By the way, I am sorry for my behavior and disrespecting you," she apologized.

"Oh, leave it. I am happy that you realized your mistake and came here to apologize," I responded.

"Thanks to you, being insulted in school, you came here to meet me and give me another chance," she acknowledged.

"I may sound rude, but it's not your fault; it was your ego that created the mess," I pointed out.

"You know what, Jeh, actually, you showed me the mirror, and now I am feeling guilty for all those students with whom I have misbehaved," she admitted.

"Flush all your thoughts and make a fresh start. There is no age or time parameter to start a new life," I advised.

"In this new journey, will you be my partner? I can't find a better guy than you," she unexpectedly proposed.

Not prepared for this googly, I suggested, "Let's go to my favorite café and talk there if comfortable."

"Ya sure, and don't worry. I am not forcing you to be my partner or to give your verdict. Take your time, and it will be totally fine if you don't want to be a partner; don't be stressed," she reassured.

"What would you prefer- Cappuccino or masala tea?" I asked.

"I am open to both options," she replied.

"Waiter... 2 Masala Tea and 2 cheesy grilled sandwiches," I ordered.

"By the time our order is coming, let's play a fun game," Shristi suggested.

"Good idea. What's the game and its rules?" I inquired.

"The game is very simple; you just have to pass me the tissue next to you, and I will write a word or a sentence, and you have to complete it and vice versa," she explained.

"Nice.... It sounds interesting; I will make the first move," I agreed.

"Please give some easy word," she requested.

"Relax, this word is very close to you. Take it," I said.

"Oh my gosh, it's literally not an easy word for me still I'll try my best to complete the game. Now your turn," she responded.

"Impressed with your answer for school, you have written guilty. Now tackle this letter," I challenged.

"It is one of the easiest words, and I was ready for this. Have it," she confidently replied.

"Excuse me, sir, here's your order," the waiter interrupted.

"Thank you. Shristi have it," I said.

"Hmm... Nice food," she remarked.

Paying the bill, I suggested, "Shall we proceed?"

"Ya sure. It's nice meeting you, and I am sorry once again. Please call me if you are comfortable," she said, leading to an awkward silence.

"Bye. Bhaiya, drop me at my place; I am ready," I quickly said.

"Bye," she responded.

Later, Vidhi asked, "Dadaji, what did you decide after the meeting? Did you call and accept her proposal?"

The *Acceptance*

I found myself caught in the crossroads of emotions, uncertain about how to respond to Shristi's unexpected proposal. Luckily, my reliable friend, Lucky, stepped in, proving the adage, "Har ek friend zaroori hota hai."

"I was not sure what to answer, and in this situation, entered Lucky. Seeing him, I understood why people say, 'Har ek friend zaroori hota hai.' On my one call, he came to my place without thinking twice," I recounted.

"Merry Christmas…. Mom made these special Christmas muffins for you," Lucky greeted as he entered.

"Say thanks to Aunty from my side, and yes, tonight you are going to stay here," I responded.

"OK, I have no issues. Now give me the treat of being a topper of the school. Order chicken kebab and chicken biryani, and yes, gulab jamun is mandatory," Lucky demanded in his usual jovial manner.

After dinner, as we sat and talked, I decided to share the events of the evening.

"Today I met her at Dada-Dadi Park," I began.

"Wow, what are you saying? I am glad that you decided to meet her. So, everything is sorted now?" Lucky inquired.

"No.... things are now more complicated," I admitted.

"Why? What happened?" Lucky questioned.

"She played Googly and requested me to be his partner. Although she is not forcing me to say yes and accept it. I can neither say yes nor can I reject her; hope you understand," I explained.

"I can totally understand your condition, but you must accept her proposal as she is good in academics, whereas you are good in socializing, so you both complement each other. How will you tell your decision to her?" Lucky suggested.

"She gave her number and said, WhatsApp me if yes," I shared.

"WhatsApp her and ask her to meet at Paradise café," Lucky advised.

I took out my phone and composed a message: "Hi Shristi, can we meet at Paradise café tomorrow afternoon?"

After a short wait, a WhatsApp notification popped up.

"Hello Mr. Jeh. Thank you so much for accepting my proposal. I will be there by 12:45 PM," Shristi responded.

Panicking a bit, I turned to Lucky for advice. "What to reply?"

"Stop panicking. Just write okay in reply," Lucky reassured.

"Don't worry; I will be there by 12:30 as I am excited to start this journey," I replied.

"Great! I like your sportsmanship," Shristi responded.

"Lovely Jeh, I liked your confidence, but please be careful of her," Lucky warned.

"Why? Why are you saying this? Initially, you were the one who suggested I meet and forgive her, and now when I am doing this, you are stopping me. Is everything okay because I know you are stopping me for a reason; what's that?" I questioned.

"I am not restricting or holding you back. I am just saying be careful as in 2 months we have our final exam and this friendship may affect your marks," Lucky explained.

"Don't worry, buddy. I know what to do, and I will be responsible for my result. Thank you for your advice," I assured him.

"By the way, what will you gift her?" Lucky asked, changing the topic.

"Gift! But why? There is no such occasion," I replied.

"Oh my god Jeh, I don't know tumhara Kya hota If I am not with you," Lucky teased.

"Now what have I done that you are scolding and taunting me?" I laughed.

"Don't you know the golden rule of meeting? Always approach the girl with a gift as this creates a good first impression in the girl's mind, and the first impression is the last impression," Lucky advised.

"Oh…. I got your point. I know what to gift her," I said.

The next morning, as I prepared for the meeting, Lucky offered his opinion. "How am I looking? I wore my favorite black shirt with a black leather jacket, topped up with sunglasses, and styled my hair with gel."

"Everything suits you, and you are just killing it. Bro, it's 12 already now leave. By the way, have you kept her gift?" Lucky asked.

"Yes, I put her gift first in my bag. I am booking a cab for the location," I replied.

"I have already booked a table for 2," Lucky informed.

A few minutes later, as Shristi appeared at the café, waving her hands in the air, I couldn't help but feel a mix of excitement and nervousness. "Hi... I saw her and fainted."

Curious, Vidhi interrupted, "Why, Dadaji, what did you see?"

The *Beginning*

"Hey Jeh, what happened? Open your eyes and take a deep breath," Shristi's concerned voice cut through the momentary silence that followed my unexpected fainting spell.

"Shit. I am sorry, I don't know how I fainted," I confessed, my embarrassment evident.

"Shhh… Calm down, it's totally fine," Shristi reassured me, her warm smile encouraging me to relax.

"Shall we order something first? I am dying of hunger," I suggested, eager to shift the focus away from my momentary lapse.

"Actually, I am hungry too. Generally, I have my lunch between 11:00-11:30 AM at my place," Shristi shared, offering a glimpse into her routine.

"Let's start the day on a sweet note. What say?" I proposed, hoping to steer the conversation towards lighter matters.

"Give me the menu, and I will order," Shristi responded, her eyes scanning the dessert offerings.

The waiter, a silent observer to our unfolding drama, approached to take our orders. Shristi's choices of a Blueberry cheesecake and a chocolate jar pastry hinted at a shared love for indulgence.

"Feeling better now?" Shristi inquired, her genuine concern putting me at ease.

"Yes. Now I know why I fainted. You are the reason," I confessed, my gaze meeting Shristi's.

"Oh really! How am I your culprit, Mr. Jeh?" Shristi teased, a playful glint in her eyes.

"Why not? You look stunning in this white dress and your long black hair, sharp cat eyes, and extended nails enhance and complement your beauty," I complimented, revealing a keen eye for detail.

Shristi blushed, her laughter echoing in the café. The waiter returned with our dessert, interrupting the flirtatious exchange.

"Excuse me, ma'am, your order," the waiter announced, placing the delectable treats before us.

"Thank you," Shristi acknowledged, her attention shifting between me and the tempting desserts.

"Anything else ma'am?" the waiter inquired.

"Shristi, pizza or pasta?" I turned to her, steering the conversation towards our impending lunch.

"Actually both. I love red sauce pasta and simple cheese pizza," she replied, signaling the waiter to take note of our additional order.

As we delved into a delightful meal, the casual banter continued. I hinted at having a surprise for Shristi, creating an air of anticipation. When the topic shifted to why I agreed to meet her, the nuances of our budding connection came to the fore.

"First, you tell me why you agreed to meet me," Shristi sought clarity, her curiosity bubbling.

"Why, any problem?" I questioned, gauging the underlying tone in Shristi's inquiry.

"No, not at all, I just want to know why you decided to be my friend," Shristi clarified, a sincerity in her eyes that mirrored my own openness.

"First of all, please stop calling me your partner; I am your friend," I emphasized, setting a tone of camaraderie. "The second most important reason that attracted me was your attitude towards competition and competitors. Now you tell me it was your proposal."

Shristi, appreciating my straightforwardness, promised to unravel the mystery behind her decision after our delightful lunch. The restaurant buzzed with the promise of shared secrets, new beginnings, and the unspoken chemistry between two souls embarking on a journey of discovery.

The *Letter*

The atmosphere in the classroom buzzed with a mix of anticipation and trepidation as our teacher unveiled the day's news. The revelation of our class-wide failure was met with apologies and promises of improvement. Amidst the gloom, our teacher lightened the mood with the announcement of a farewell party on February 5th, marking the end of an academic era.

On the much-anticipated farewell day, the festive ambiance captivated us. Lucky, my friend, observed the intricate arrangements by the juniors and noticed me lost in thought.

"Nice arrangement by our juniors. What happened? What are you thinking?" Lucky inquired, breaking my reverie.

"Ah, nothing," I replied, my mind seemingly occupied.

Vaishali, another classmate, approached us, sensing my contemplation. "I know you are waiting for Shristi. I also know you want to confess your feelings to her, but she has a strain and can't come today for the party."

My anticipation heightened as Vaishali handed me a letter from Shristi. With a mixture of excitement and apprehension, I unfolded the letter and began reading Shristi's words.

"Hi Jeh, I am glad to be your friend. It's fun studying together, and I wish you all the success you deserve. This is my last letter to you, as I am changing schools for better education." Yours truly, Shristi.

As I absorbed the contents of the letter, my thoughts raced, contemplating the significance of Shristi's departure. Questions lingered, but answers were yet to unfold.

The following day, Shristi and I agreed to meet at our familiar spot. Shristi, still nursing her injury, arrived with her driver, ready to share a revelation.

The air was thick with unspoken emotions as we faced each other.

"Hey... Still punctual and on time, hmm," I greeted, attempting to lighten the mood.

"I came here with my driver and will leave in 15 minutes. I just want to say I love you," Shristi confessed, breaking the silence.

After a brief pause, I grappled with my own feelings. "I love you too, but I fear missing a good friend. I am sorry; I don't know when and how I fell in love with you."

Shristi, with a reassuring smile, urged me not to feel guilty. "Please don't feel guilty; it's not your fault. By the way, promise me that you will forgive me for all my mistakes."

I, embracing the warmth of the moment, invoked the essence of our friendship. "Come on Senorita, 'dosti mein no sorry no thank you'."

Shristi burst into laughter, sealing the moment with a gentle kiss. "This is the final goodbye."

As Vidhi, my granddaughter, listened to this tale, curiosity and wonder filled her young eyes. "If she left the school, how did you meet and marry her?"

"Calm down and relax, Vidhi. Many more twists and turns yet to come in this story," I assured, leaving the lingering promise of a story far from its conclusion.

The *Destiny*

After bidding farewell to the familiar halls of my school, I ventured into a new chapter of my academic journey at I.I.T. Mumbai. The initial days were marked by homesickness and a desire to abandon this newfound independence. Hostel life, however, revealed its silver lining as I found an unexpected kinship among the residents of Hostel Number 4, humorously labeled the "losers."

A born actor, I discovered my sanctuary in the college's theatre, swiftly ascending to the role of the drama club president. Despite the challenging start, Hostel Number 4 became a hub for lasting connections, fostering a sense of pride within the "losers" gang.

One stormy night, under the veil of darkness, my friends and I embarked on a road trip to Nasik, a journey etched in memories. The overcast conditions altered our plans, prolonging our stay and fortifying the bonds of camaraderie.

As Amir proposed a bonfire and games for the night, we eagerly agreed. Amir, familiar with an ideal location, suggested a place dedicated to camping, complete with a tent, sleeping bags, a crackling fire, and an abundance of food—all for a modest sum of Rs 500 per person.

With a feast laid before us, we indulged in the warmth of the fire and savory delights. Tracy, instigator of the night's entertainment, proposed a game of truth or dare to elevate the excitement.

"Before igniting the fire, let's cool our stomach's fire with this tempting stuff," Tracy suggested as the aroma of the food enveloped us.

Amir assured me that everything would be managed, as the game commenced with heightened spirits. The rotating bottle pointed at me, leading to a daring challenge: to convince nearby girls to join our revelry.

Ever the charmer, I successfully persuaded the girls to participate. Among them was Aisha, whose uncanny resemblance to my school friend, Shristi, sparked a sense of nostalgia.

As Aisha revealed her connection to Shristi, my excitement reached new heights. A few days later, I reunited with Shristi, igniting memories of our school days.

"Hi Shristi, remember me, it's me, Jeh," I greeted, and the floodgates of recollection opened.

The unexpected reunion filled me with joy. "Our friendship journey starts with a fight, remember?"

Shristi, embracing me, reminisced about the past. "Oh yes. How can I forget you, Jeh? Which year are you in?"

"I'm in the 2nd year, and today, I got teleported to heaven," I exclaimed, my joy evident.

Our paths, once intertwined by destiny, converged once more. The following day, with a heart brimming with emotions, I planned to express my feelings to Shristi.

"Hey Jeh, I want to tell you something, but before that, promise me one thing," Shristi requested.

I, coolly chewing gum, replied, "Ok, I promise."

Taking a deep breath, Shristi confessed, "I love you. Will you hold my hands and be with me forever? I fell in love with you from our first meeting, and for me, it was love at first sight."

Ecstatic, I responded with an emphatic "Yes." The conditions were set—no breaking of our friendship for any reason. Our love story blossomed, with plans for marriage after final exams and securing jobs.

Vidhi, wiping away tears, couldn't contain her curiosity. "At what age did you marry? What happened to Grandmom, and why did she leave us?"

As the tale unfolded, the web of love, separation, and reunion grew more intricate, leaving Vidhi yearning for the next chapter in this captivating family saga.

The *Last Ride*

The sun dipped below the horizon as the waves whispered secrets on the beach. My heart, laden with joy, awaited Shristi's arrival.

"Hi Shristi, guess what, I am extremely happy today," I exclaimed, my eyes gleaming with excitement.

Shristi, intrigued, replied, "Oh really, that's good, but why?"

I, unable to contain my elation, shared the news, "I got placed in my dream company with an annual package of INR 1.5 crore, and next month I have to shift to Bangalore."

Shristi, thrilled for my success, responded, "Superb… So proud of you. I too have good news for you."

"Seriously, tell me fast. I am so excited," I urged.

With a beaming smile, Shristi revealed, "I too got placed in your company and am coming with you but at a lower level. I am designated for the post of senior sales executive."

Overflowing with joy, I embraced Shristi. "Congratulations, love. For me, your post doesn't matter; everything that matters is only you. This is a clear indication of destiny. Congratulations once again; so proud to be your partner."

As our lips met in a kiss, laughter echoed, marking the beginning of a new chapter. One year later, we faced the trials of parenthood, navigating through tests and doctor visits.

"Hello, Shristi, get ready fast for your tests. I am coming, and I will not entertain any excuses today. I'll be at your place in 15 minutes, so get ready like a good girl," I declared over the phone.

"Concentrate on your driving, please," Shristi teased.

Arriving promptly, I whisked Shristi to the renowned Dr. Radhika, Asia's best gynecologist. Concern etched on my face, I explained Shristi's symptoms, seeking answers to the mysterious ailments.

Dr. Radhika, examining the reports, dropped a bombshell. "Congratulations, Jeh, you are going to become a father. Shristi is 2 months pregnant."

I, a whirlwind of emotions, struggled to comprehend the news. Back home, Lucky, the ever-reliable friend, provided counsel. "First, marry her as soon as possible and then tell her the condition."

The same day, adorned with a diamond ring, I proposed to Shristi. The news of impending parenthood was delivered delicately, sparking a mix of emotions.

"Take your time and make your decision. I am with you in all conditions," I assured Shristi.

"I will keep this baby. We are going to marry tomorrow at our nearest temple," Shristi declared, sealing our commitment.

However, another twist awaited me. A mysterious phone call from my manager shattered the tranquility. Jobless and grappling with uncertainty, I hesitated, revealing the news to Shristi.

"Hello, who's this?" I answered the call.

"It's me, your manager. You have been fired, and no need to come from tomorrow," came the curt response.

Devastated, I confronted Shristi in the temple, urging her to reconsider our future. To my surprise, Shristi unveiled the truth – a prank orchestrated by Lucky.

In the months that followed, Shristi's pregnancy progressed, weaving dreams of the family we were about to create. However, life's unpredictable nature struck once again.

"I am not feeling well. I am facing difficulty in breathing," Shristi revealed one day, her demeanor hinting at a deeper struggle.

Undeterred, I suggested a long drive, hoping to fulfill Shristi's last wish. However, the journey took an unexpected turn, leading us to the hospital.

"Promise me you will always take care of our child and won't marry again," Shristi whispered, her voice frail.

In the blink of an eye, I found myself grappling with the harsh reality of life and death. The beach, once witness to our joy, now bore witness to sorrow.

"Congratulations, Mr. Jeh, it's a baby boy," Dr. Radhika announced.

Yet, amidst the joy of new life, I confronted the profound loss of my beloved Shristi.

"Dadaji, I promise, I will make you famous forever," Vidhi vowed, her tears blending with the crashing waves.

As I grappled with the juxtaposition of joy and sorrow, life's tapestry unfolded, leaving Vidhi and Vivan to navigate its twists and turns, cherishing the memories of a love that transcended the boundaries of time.

www.ingramcontent.com/pod-product-compliance
Lightning Source LLC
LaVergne TN
LVHW061605070526
838199LV00077B/7177